WINTER'S BLACK CHRISTMAS

A WINTER BLACK CHRISTMAS MYSTERY

MARY STONE

Copyright © 2021 by Mary Stone

All rights reserved.

No part of this book may be reproduced in any form or by any electronic or mechanical means, including information storage and retrieval systems, without written permission from the author, except for the use of brief quotations in a book review.

❦ Created with Vellum

While Christmas is the most glorious time of the year, the season brings sadness and pain for many. This story is dedicated to those who celebrate with good cheer and to those whose only wish is for the day to be over. Much love and peace to you all.

DESCRIPTION

Jingle all the way...to murder.

When FBI Special Agent Winter Black enters a luxurious Montana cabin two days before Christmas, she's excited because all the people she loves will be joining her soon. Her joy is dashed when an unexpected blizzard hits the area, leaving her stranded and without any means of communication.

And she's not alone.

Instead of her friends and family arriving, a momma cat shows up at the cabin's door, begging for help. Braving the snow, Winter finds more than just the feline's litter.

She finds a dead body.

With nowhere to run and thrust into a game of psychological warfare by a killer she can't see, Winter's hope for a bright and shiny Christmas turns into a fight for her life.

Winter's Black Christmas by Mary Stone, is a reminder that both dreams and nightmares come from the same place...your mind.

1

"'Tis the season to have a nervous breakdown, fa la la la la, la la…la…oh wow."

Winter Black stared at the enormous cabin sitting almost like a wood and glass castle on the side of the snow-covered mountain. Her mouth sagged open as she gaped at the home's size and grandeur. And that view. "Wow" was the only word that came to mind.

"Toto, I'm not in Virginia anymore."

Actually, was she even at the right place? Winter pulled her rented Jeep Grand Cherokee up a few more yards to inspect the equally grand mailbox more closely.

1891 Heaven's View Road

Yes, this was it. Heaven's View. And boy, the name wasn't lying. It might have been an understatement of dramatic proportions.

Winter had seen pictures of the place—how could anyone call this behemoth a cabin?—of course, because she'd been the one to secure the rental, but as she pulled into the gravel driveway and moved forward, she was still in awe. The images on the website didn't do the structure before her justice.

From the website, Winter learned that the ten thousand-square foot house sat on only an acre of land, but that land abutted nearly a hundred acres of open space. The man she'd spoken to about securing the rental had promised that she wouldn't see another human being for miles.

It was a lot of cabin for just one person, she knew, but she'd only be alone for today. Tomorrow, on Christmas Eve, the love of her life, Noah Dalton, would be coming, bringing Winter's beloved grandparents with him. And, equally as exciting, Noah's mom, stepdad, and sister would be joining them the day after Christmas, as would Autumn Trent and Aiden Parrish, Winter's closest friends from the FBI.

This would be the first time all the people Winter and Noah loved most would be under the same roof, which was why Winter had made a point to arrive before everyone else. She wanted everything to be perfect.

Pulling to a stop in front of one of the four garage doors, Winter was quick to get out of the Jeep and even quicker to snatch the heavy coat from the passenger seat.

It was freezing.

Richmond, Virginia had been a brisk fifty-seven degrees when Noah had dropped her off at the airport that morning. At the time, she'd complained about how chilly it was.

"And Montana said, 'Hold my beer.'"

Clouds of vapor escaped her mouth with the words, making her smile grow wider. Winter inhaled deeply, breathing in the twenty-degree air like it had the power to cleanse her of every negative thought she'd ever had.

Of which, she'd had plenty.

"Nope...not trotting down memory lane today."

Managing to tear her gaze from the home, Winter turned to face the expanse of mountain ridges stretching as far as she could see. Sharp peaks bright with snow towered toward a sky just beginning to hint at the oranges, yellows, and reds of the coming sunset.

And Winter had only *thought* this place couldn't be more beautiful. If she'd been warmer with little to do, she would have stood there until the sun completely disappeared.

She glanced at her watch. It wasn't quite four-thirty yet and already getting dark. She still needed to unpack the Jeep and then start on the long checklist she'd been working on all month. But first...

"Hello!"

Hello...hello...hello...

Winter smiled as the echo returned her greeting for several seconds. She was tempted to yell again, but a gust of wind stung her cheeks and whipped her black hair around her face and into her eyes.

Crunch.

A sound caught her attention, and Winter stilled. Mr. Mills, the property manager she'd spoken to, had promised there would be no other people nearby. He'd said nothing about mammals of other kinds.

Bears would be in hibernation, surely, but there were other creatures roaming this forest. Moose, elk...mountain lions.

Crunch. Crunch. Crunch.

"Time to go."

As a special agent with the Federal Bureau of Investigation, Winter might carry a badge and a gun, but her ego wasn't so big that she felt comfortable going head-to-head with a giant moose or a two-hundred-pound cat with four-inch teeth.

Winter fought a different type of animal in her job, and she wouldn't hesitate to pull the trigger if one of the men and women she chased stepped out of the forest. Wildlife was different. She was currently encroaching on their turf, and they were just doing what animals did. She respected them too much to be the one to cause them to be maimed or killed. Winter would hate like crazy to have to shoot an animal to save her own life.

She would, of course. She would because, after living the past thirteen years with a cloud over her head, she was determined to step out into the sun. To enjoy life. To love hard. To give back to the world more than she took.

To no longer live with shame and guilt as her constant companion. And rage. So much rage.

"Okey dokey." Her voice held a singsong quality that wasn't in her normal repertoire of tones. Was she getting altitude sickness? "How about we focus on good cheer and tidings for a while? Can we do that, please?"

Crunch. Crunch. Crunch.

The sound was louder now, and as Winter searched the woods, the hair raised on the back of her neck. Goose bumps that weren't solely from the cold prickled her arms.

Winter was being watched. She could feel it. The question was…from what? Or by whom?

Straightening her shoulders, Winter lifted her hands to make a megaphone of her mouth. "Who's there?"

There…there…there…

She didn't smile at the echo this time as every sense she possessed focused on the area surrounding her. Evergreen trees tipped with snow so white it hurt her eyes. Wind whistling softly through branches. Fresh air so cold it burned her lungs.

Crunch.

Resolve shattering like an icicle falling onto a rock, Winter turned and hurried to the house. The feeling of being heavily scrutinized didn't falter as she high-stepped it up the stairs to the front porch, being careful to avoid the icy patches clinging to the wood.

Under the enormous shelter dotted with swings and rocking chairs, Winter turned back and faced the view again, searching the woods for the thing that had made her so jumpy. Her gaze was pulled to the magnificence before her, though.

"Oh my...wow."

The vast expanse of mountain and sky was even more breathtaking this time, the sun appearing to be only inches above the tallest peak. The explosion of color was too beautiful for words.

Scattering.

That was the official name of the phenomenon, Noah once told her. When she'd seemed impressed by his meteorological knowledge, he'd gone on to explain that molecules and small particles in the atmosphere changed the direction of light rays, causing them to scatter. When the sun was low on the horizon, sunlight passed through more air, transforming the sky into an array of yellows, oranges, and reds.

As Winter watched the sky change before her eyes, she forgot about the unease she'd felt only minutes before. With each heartbeat, the sun sank closer to the edge of the world, becoming redder.

"Red has the longest wavelength of any visible light," Noah had told her that peaceful evening. *"That's why the sun is red when it's on the horizon. Its long path through the atmosphere blocks all other colors."*

When the sun was only an inch or so from disappearing, the red transformed into the same shade Winter saw when her special ability insisted she zone in on something important. The same special ability "gifted" to her by the man who'd killed her parents, kidnapped her brother, and left her for dead.

The Preacher.

The wind picked up, as if frightened by even the thought of the serial killer who'd murdered so many. Winter didn't blame it. Douglas Kilroy had been a terrifying man.

Had.

Winter had hunted him down, making sure he never had the opportunity to hurt another innocent soul. She'd been too late, of course. The Preacher had been given plenty of time to inflict more damage, ensuring Winter's baby brother was well trained to fill his shoes.

"Why are you even thinking about him right now? Of them?"

Even as she voiced the frustrated questions, Winter knew why.

No corner of Earth was safe from evil. Even in a place as exquisite as this.

As the sun kissed the mountaintop, she resolved to push all unhappy thoughts from her mind. She would drink her first spiked eggnog, kiss under the mistletoe, sing carols so loud it hurt her throat.

This was going to be the best Christmas of her twenty-six years of life. Nothing bad could touch her in this magical place with the wonderful people who would soon be joining her.

Crunch.

Winter hurried to the front door.

2

4-3-2-8-3-6

Winter made short work of tapping in the numbers and retrieving a key nestled inside the lockbox. She still couldn't believe the code was the numerical equivalent to HEAVEN.

"If you ever forget the code, just look at your phone," Mr. Mills had told her with a jolly laugh. "That'll help jog your memory every time."

Winter hadn't been as amused. That seemed like a significant security issue to her. "Does the code ever change?"

Another long round of chuckles. "No need, my dear. Mr. Worthington only allows those of the highest caliber to have access to his cabin." He lowered his voice. "And I believe Beyoncé is Christmasing at home this year. The twins didn't want Santa to have trouble locating them, you see."

He'd been kidding...right?

That's what she'd thought at first, but now, gazing at the luxurious interior, she wasn't so sure.

Of course he was. Or else she would have never made the "highest caliber" list to stay here. Not that she'd been the one to have this connection to Mr. Seymour Worthington in the first place. That would have been courtesy of Special Supervisory Agent Aiden Parrish, who had been friends with the billionaire for years.

Winter needed friends like that.

Actually, no she didn't. She was perfectly content with the friends she currently had. The friends who would all be here this weekend.

With a final look out the glass door to see if she could spot anything moving outside, Winter twisted the lock and pocketed the key. The main room was surprisingly warm, but that could have been because she'd gawked at the sun setting for so long she'd turned into a human popsicle. Opening her new leather shoulder bag—an early Christmas present to herself—she pulled out the checklist Mr. Mills had emailed her.

Code to the door—check.

Garage door openers will be found in the top drawer of the chiffonier.

"What the ho ho ho is a chiffonier?" Winter glanced around at all the oversized pieces of furniture in the room. "Come on, you're a special agent. Figure it out."

"Drawer" was her first clue while "top" was her second, so she headed to the first piece of furniture with more than one drawer. The antique wood of what she would have called a chest of drawers squeaked when she pulled it open.

Bingo.

"Winter Black, special agent extraordinaire." She rolled her eyes at herself before snatching up one of the little black boxes and tucking it into her coat pocket. She went back to her checklist.

Please note that the temperature in each section of the cabin will be set to precisely sixty-two degrees. Upon vacating the resi-

dence, please return temperature to that setting. You'll find the control tablet in the second drawer of the chiffonier.

Another squeaky drawer revealed a sleek tablet that, when touched, exposed a slew of settings for everything from music to lighting and temperature to window blinds.

She moved to the closest floor-to-ceiling window and gasped. The sky was painted in blood. At least, that was the first thought to come to her mind.

"Red sky at night, sailors' delight," she murmured as she fiddled with the controls for the blinds, ultimately deciding to leave them up. Spooked or not, she couldn't make herself block that view.

Scrolling to the temperature, she frowned. She'd thought it felt much warmer than sixty-two inside, and she wasn't wrong. The device stated that each section of the home was currently set to a cozy seventy-four.

"Uh-oh. Someone's in trouble."

The singsong quality in her voice was back. Altitude sickness. It had to be.

Finding the screen that controlled the lights, she located the great room, kitchen, and garage, turning them on full strength. She'd play with the colors and dim settings later. Right now, she needed to get to work.

A few minutes later, she'd braved the cold and the spooks to pull the Jeep into the garage closest to the kitchen, keeping the vehicle locked until the door was fully closed. Mentally berating herself for being so easily frightened, she began the chore of unloading the abundance of luggage she'd brought with her. She'd had to pay the ridiculous extra charges at the airport, but she hadn't minded too much.

Bringing ornaments and other decorations with her seemed smarter than attempting to find ones she loved a couple days before Christmas in an area she wasn't familiar with. Plus, she'd already been told there was a small store at the base of the mountain. If she wanted anything unique, she'd have to drive all the way back down to Bozeman.

In the great room, she opened the large box marked as "fragile," praying that the baggage handlers had paid attention to the warning. Breath held, she pulled out the layers of bubble wrap, happy to see that each glass ball was intact, as were the delicate angels she'd fallen in love with at a little antique store her best friend Autumn Trent had introduced her to.

"Congratulations. You don't have to kill a baggage handler today." She stood and turned in a circle. Now, all she needed was the tree.

Where was it?

Leaving all her luggage in the great room, Winter began wandering through the cabin, deciding that it was finally time for the grand tour of the home. The polished wooden floors gleamed as she explored, making her way to the kitchen to more properly appreciate the black marble countertops.

She didn't find the Christmas tree she'd ordered. What she did find was mildly disturbing. Two dirty bowls and spoons were in the sink.

Winter inspected the kitchen more closely. There were crumbs on the marble and the floor, with what looked like a smear of peanut butter coating a drawer handle.

"You have got to be kidding me."

Mr. Mills had assured her the cabin would be thoroughly cleaned prior to her arrival. Winter wasn't a neatnik by any stretch of the imagination, but this wasn't even what *she'd* describe as clean. Moving down the hallway, she began opening doors, not stopping until she found what must have been the master suite.

The bed was made but not very neatly. In fact, it more closely resembled the way Winter made her own bed when she was late for work, pulling the blankets up to cover the pillows and calling it good enough.

In the master suite, there was a spot of toothpaste in the sink and several brown hairs in the bottom of the shower. A used towel was tossed over a bar attached to the wall. Wrinkling her nose, she reached out and touched the cotton. It was dry.

But still...yuck.

Growing angry, Winter marched throughout the rest of the cabin, searching for additional signs that the housekeeper hadn't fulfilled her duties. There was dirt on the floor by the back door and a few brown leaves on the rug.

None of the other bedrooms appeared to have been used, which was a blessing, and the upstairs gleamed. Overall, the place looked good except for the main parts of the house.

And where in the world was the Christmas tree?

Reaching into her shoulder bag, she pulled out her phone, preparing to toss a few questions at the delightful Mr. Mills like darts.

No service.

Seriously?

Holding the phone over her head, she moved around the cabin, watching the screen in hopes of finding exactly the right spot in which a single bar would appear. Nope. Not downstairs or upstairs, either.

Tossing the phone on the leather sofa, Winter plopped down beside it.

What to do?

Pulling out the checklist Mr. Mills sent her, she found the information she needed about the Wi-Fi code.

Cell phone service can be spotty in the area. Winter snorted. Was "spotty" slang for nonexistent in this neck of the woods?

You may connect to our complimentary Wi-Fi. Winter snorted again, louder this time. Based on the weekly rate of this cabin, the dang internet *should* be free. If four different families weren't chipping in for the cost, she would have never been able to afford such luxury on her government salary. And that was *after* the "friend of Aiden" discount. *The network is called View Heaven, and the password is H3av3n$Gat3.*

Winter barely refrained from yet another snort. A third grader could see through that code. "Mr. Billionaire should care more about security than he does about the number of garages he has." Since the man had given them a pretty good discount, she'd type a list of suggestions to make this multi-million-dollar home more secure.

After the New Year. They'd be staying here until January second.

Staring at her phone, she watched the circle spin around and around…and around. *No network detected.*

Great. She tried again, moving to the back of the house this time. *No network detected.*

She'd spotted an office earlier, so she headed there next, thinking it would be the obvious place for the internet equipment. Nope. She opened every drawer and cabinet but found nothing coming close to even resembling a modem.

"Come on, special powers." She tapped her temples, hoping to activate the mysterious synaptic connections that made her brain different from the other eight billion people on Earth. No such luck.

It truly stank to have an ability that only worked when it wanted to, and more often than not made her physically ill. In addition to possessing the strange sixth sense that created a red haze over objects that needed her attention, she also received occasional visions that drained her energy and brought a trickle of blood from her nose while her brain felt like it was going to explode.

When it became clear that her "powers" didn't plan on helping, she went through all six bedrooms again, this time opening closets and anything else that could hide a Wi-Fi router. Disappointed, she dropped back on the leather couch in the great room and stared into the blackness beyond the windows.

Was something staring back?

As warm as she was, she shivered. "Stop it." She refused to psych herself out once again. And besides, she still had so much to do to create a bright and shiny Christmas.

There was a little store, she remembered, a few miles down the mountain. Though she hadn't planned on going out after dark, her current circumstances had other ideas.

Pushing to her feet, she grabbed her shoulder bag and keys. After bundling up in extra layers, she was going to call Mr. Mills and get the housekeeping situation figured out.

And find her Christmas tree.

3

The little general store might have only been a few miles away as the crow flies, but it took Winter almost twenty minutes to creep down the steep and curvy mountain. Even though the Jeep was four-wheel drive, many of the turns were precarious, making her feel like she was on the edge of a black abyss.

On top of that, there were many slick places, especially where trees shaded the road from the sun. It had only taken a couple slides for Winter to slow to a crawl. Winter's fingers ached from gripping the steering wheel so tight, and she allowed herself a few minutes to stretch her hands and relax before making her phone call.

Mr. Mills answered right away. "Ms. Black, so good to hear from you so soon. Have you caught your breath yet after beholding the beauty of Heaven's View?"

Winter rolled her head on her neck, wincing when it popped several times. "Both the cabin and view are even better than expected, but I do have a couple problems I could use your help with."

Mr. Mills made a sound that was very close to a gasp. "A

problem? Dear me. Yes, please do share these problems so they can be rectified right away."

Rolling her head in the other direction, Winter collected her thoughts. Mr. Mills was much too nice for her to come at him with both barrels blazing. "First, I'm afraid that your housekeeper's attention to detail might not be what it should." Mr. Mills gasped again, but Winter went on before he could interrupt. "And the Christmas tree I needed delivered today hasn't arrived. Lastly, the Wi-Fi isn't working. Do you know where the router is located?"

Silence.

Winter checked that the call hadn't been disconnected. "Mr. Mills?"

"Yes…oh, yes, dear. I'm here. So sorry, but you've caught me quite by surprise. Let's see, I'll answer your questions beginning with the Wi-Fi issue if that's agreeable with you."

The man was so formal, she imagined him with a British accent. "That's quite agreeable, Mr. Mills."

"The Wi-Fi router is located in the garage closet, in the cabinet closest to the circuit breaker box."

Seriously? The garage was the last place she'd ever think to search.

"Perfect. I'll look there when I get back."

"Get back from where, dear?"

None of your business. Winter bit back the automatic reply and inhaled deeply. "My cell phone won't receive a signal, so I drove to the general store to place this call."

"I see. Well, I'm sure a quick reboot of the system should get you straight back in the communication loop. Now, on to the housekeeping issues and the missing Christmas tree. I spoke to Mrs. Ralston just last week. She assured me that the cabin would be spotless and that she would personally choose the perfect ten-foot specimen and have it delivered today."

Winter scrubbed a hand down her face. Perfect specimen? If Mr. Mills hadn't possessed a Montanan accent, she would have pegged him as a British gent for sure.

"I'm sure Mrs. Ralston is very capable and lovely, but I'm sorry to say that the master bedroom's bed appears to have been slept in, and there is toothpaste and hair in the master bath. Dirty dishes are in the sink, and there are dirt and leaves by the back door."

Silence.

Oh yeah… "And there is no Christmas tree."

More silence.

"Mr. Mills?"

"Y-yes, dear. Forgive me, but I'm truly stunned. That degree of uncleanliness is unacceptable, and I'll get to the bottom of this at once. May I call you back in a few moments?"

"Sure. I'll explore the general store and pick up a few extra supplies."

"If Deborah has any of her fresh apple turnovers, you'd be doing yourself a service by buying several."

Winter attempted to suffuse warmth into her tone. "I'll be on the lookout. Looking forward to hearing from you soon."

A bell clanged on the door as Winter opened the door of the general store. Stomping little bits of snow from her boots before stepping inside, Winter pulled off her gloves and stuffed them into her pockets. The building was cozy and warm and smelled of something made of cinnamon that was so strong it made Winter's eyes burn. There were no shopping carts to be seen, so she settled on a wicker basket that shouted, *"Fill me up!"* on the side.

The store was mostly empty save for an enormous man in a bright red flannel shirt. He appeared to smile, but it was hard to tell with the shaggy chest-length beard obscuring most of his face. His eyes didn't smile, though, and she held his gaze with a hard one of her own when his pink tongue poked through the facial hair, fluttering in her direction.

Um...gross.

Winter shifted her leather shoulder bag, opening the top so that her arsenal of weapons would be within easy reach. Her Glock was there, in addition to a stun gun and can of pepper spray. Though the stranger easily outweighed her by a hundred pounds, she didn't feel at a disadvantage.

"May I help you?"

Winter whirled, her hand instinctively going to where her gun was normally holstered. Instead of a raging lunatic, a pint-sized woman stood behind her. She laughed, her hand moving up to cover her heart. "Sorry. You startled me."

The woman possessed such a hunchback that she was forced to turn her head to the side to look up at Winter. "Quiet as a mouse, my daddy always said." Her smile was beautiful, as was the pure white hair pulled back into a tight bun. "Are you needing anything specific? I'm happy to point you in the right direction if you are. I'm Deborah, by the way."

Ah...the apple turnover-making Deborah, Winter assumed.

"I'm actually waiting on a phone call." Winter waved the device in her hand as if it were some kind of proof. "There's no cell signal at the cabin I'm renting, so I thought I'd come here, place my call, and pick up a few supplies."

The clerk nodded her understanding. "The storm is hitting quite a bit earlier and harder than expected. Clouds seem to act like brick walls when that happens around here."

Storm?

Winter licked her lips. "What storm? I looked at the forecast just this morning, and they were calling for a couple inches of snow but said nothing about a storm."

The small woman waved a hand. "Fool me once, shame

on you. Fool me twice, shame on me. Fool me thirty-five thousand eight hundred and sixty-two times, shame on the weatherman."

Winter would have laughed had her brain not been spiraling out of control. "How bad is this storm supposed to be?"

Deborah made a movement that Winter supposed was a shrug. "A foot or so, they're saying. But from the looks of the sky, I wouldn't be surprised if it wasn't closer to two."

Two. Feet. Of. Snow.

Was this elderly Tinkerbell of a woman pulling her leg?

"Are you serious?" Winter began tapping at her phone, finding the weather app within seconds. And there it was, a flashing red warning sign, and something about an unexpected warm pressure pushing an unexpected cold pressure into an unexpected circle that looked very much like the hurricanes that tended to blast the East Coast.

Unexpected?

With all the multibillion-dollar gadgets meteorologists controlled, how in the world did anything weather related come as a surprise?

"We're going to close up a bit early today, dear, so if you'll be needing anything, now's a good time to be selecting."

Winter got the hint.

"Well, I've heard a rumor that your apple turnovers are the best I'll ever eat."

That beautiful beaming smile returned, and a rosy hue crept up the little woman's cheeks as she scurried over to a counter. "You're in luck. I have half a dozen left."

Winter simply couldn't resist. "I'll take them all."

If she didn't eat them, she knew an always hungry special agent who would. She glanced out the window, frowning at the snow falling on the other side. She just hoped the storm wouldn't be strong enough to keep everyone from joining her.

While Deborah bagged the pastries, Winter moved through the rows of shelves to the refrigerated area, being careful of the flannel wearing man still leering at her. Knowing how isolated she would be, she'd planned ahead and had ordered most of the groceries she would need from a large grocery chain with a promise that they'd be delivered tomorrow morning.

But if a big storm was coming, would that delivery be delayed or canceled? Or did Montanans simply go about their business during a blizzard? She started tossing some basic staples into her basket, just to be safe.

Milk, butter, eggs, bacon, bread. Peanut butter and jelly. Ham and cheese. Coffee...the largest container they had. Sugar. She spotted a box of hot chocolate and snatched it up too.

This should do.

Just as she arrived at the checkout desk, her phone chimed. Smiling an apology to Deborah, she took the call.

"Hello, Mr. Mills. I hope you're calling with good news."

"My dear, I truly wish I were."

Winter's stomach cramped. "That doesn't sound good."

"I'm afraid I was unable to get in touch with Mrs. Ralston, and when I called the Christmas tree farm, they didn't have an order for your delivery."

Winter groaned but cycled through her options. "I can clean the cabin myself, I suppose." She headed to the cleaning aisle to pick up those additional supplies.

"I'll deduct twenty percent from your bill for that trouble."

"Thank you. Could you also call the farm back and ask for a tree to be delivered tomorrow?"

"Well...about that." Mr. Mill's tone turned sorrowful, and

Winter closed her eyes. "I'm afraid an unexpected snowstorm may interfere with any deliveries tomorrow. Our road maintenance crews are excellent at staying ahead of the snow on well-traveled roads, but..."

"But the road to Heaven's View isn't well-traveled," Winter finished for him.

"That's correct, my dear. The storm is supposed to be past your area by noon tomorrow, but since it is also Christmas Eve, the farm will be closing early." He sighed. "I'm terribly sorry that Mrs. Ralston has failed you so badly."

As Mr. Mills spoke, Winter's mind turned to something more important than a tree that might not get delivered.

"Mr. Mills, do you know if this storm will be powerful enough to cause flights to be canceled or delayed tomorrow?"

He made a humming sound. "I'm not quite certain, my dear, but if we get the amount of snow the forecasters are warning of, delays will be the least of it."

That was what she'd been afraid he'd say. "Okay, thank you. I'm going to head back before the storm begins."

"Do be careful, my dear. The mountain gets treacherous more quickly than you're likely used to. Use caution."

"Thank you. I will."

After thanking the sweet shopkeeper and eyeing the man in flannel to make sure he didn't follow her, Winter carried her groceries to the Jeep. She sighed as her hope for a bright and shiny Christmas grew dimmer.

4

"Darlin', it'll be okay." Noah's voice was as soothing as warm milk over the Jeep's sound system. "I'll get us to you if I have to carry Beth and Jack up that mountain myself."

Winter took a huge bite of apple turnover, using the excuse of chewing to delay the need to answer. She was near tears, which made her mad. For a woman who rarely cried, getting emotional over a stupid holiday was ridiculous.

Except this wasn't a stupid holiday at all. This was supposed to be perfect. The first time in thirteen years that she didn't long for the family that had been lost to her so long ago.

Gramma Beth and Grampa Jack couldn't have been more wonderful to Winter when they took her in as an emotionally and physically stunted thirteen-year-old. The parents of her slaughtered mother, they'd both fought through their own grief to care for their granddaughter the best they could. They'd done well, and she loved them dearly, but...

But what?

But deep in her heart, she'd longed for a table full of

people and laughter that had been stripped from her by the whim of The Preacher. She'd wanted more, even though she didn't think she entirely deserved it.

Maybe the universe agreed.

She shook off that depressing thought.

"Darlin', are you there?"

Winter swallowed the delicious bite of cinnamon and apple. "Yeah. It will be fine, I'm sure. Montana expects big snows like this, and I'm sure they have the equipment to take care of it. Will you call Gramma and Grampa and let them know about the possible delay?"

"Of course. I'll let Mom, Autumn, and Aiden know too, though they probably won't be affected since they're all coming the day after Christmas."

"Thank you." As she took another bite of the pastry, snowflakes nearly the size of her hand began to fall. "Oh wow."

"What?"

Winter chewed quickly and swallowed so she didn't have to try to talk around a mouthful of dough and fruit. "It's snowing, and I don't think I've ever seen flakes this big."

"You better head back to the cabin then." Noah's voice was now tinged with concern.

She patted the Jeep's heated steering wheel. "I've got four-wheel drive in this sexy beast of a vehicle."

He laughed, but it sounded strained. "If the road is as steep and curvy as you said, four-wheel drive or not, don't push your luck."

Noah was right. Her luck hadn't been that great to start with.

Stuffing the remainder of the turnover back into its sack, she put the vehicle in neutral before pressing the 4WD LOW button as the rental car rep had told her to do. The light came on and she relaxed a little. At least something was working as it was supposed to.

"I'm heading off but stay with me so I'll know how far the signal goes."

Noah laughed, the sound rich and warm. "Darlin', I'm always with you."

Tears threatened again because she knew it was true.

Winter had become an FBI agent not out of the spirit of fighting crime but to avenge her parents and hopefully learn what had happened to her baby brother. On her path to vengeance, she hadn't been the most loving person in the world.

Noah had been assigned as her partner and had shouldered the brunt of her intense focus on justice with a resiliency and humor she'd begun to trust. He'd had her back long before he had her heart, and the only fear she had in their relationship was that she would never, ever deserve him.

"I'm with you too." Winter cleared her throat of the emotion wanting to grip it. "Have you packed yet?"

Another warm laugh. "You're kidding me, right?"

That pulled a grin from her. Noah had what could only be a man's ability to toss everything he needed into the tiniest of bags five minutes before hitting the door.

"I didn't think so, but mostly because I think I packed about everything else in the apartment."

It was true. Two huge suitcases, a carry-on bag, and the box of Christmas ornaments had cost her an additional hundred bucks to get here. In fairness, though, one of the suitcases was filled with nothing but presents that she'd bought and wrapped after watching YouTube videos to learn fancy ways to tie pretty ribbons. And to ensure the corners didn't look like a five-year-old had done the wrapping.

Whew, she needed a wife.

As exhausting as it had been, she'd actually loved each of those tasks more than she'd ever admit in public. And she'd secretly bought a dress for Christmas dinner that wasn't some shade of gray or solid black. She couldn't wait to see the look on Noah's face when she paraded out in fire engine red.

If he could get here.

"So far so good," she said as she took the first steep curve that went straight up what seemed to be a forty-degree hill. "Can you still hear me?"

"I hear you, darlin', and in case I lose you, remember that I love you and I'll be there as soon as I can, Gramma and Grampa in tow. We're going to have a wonderful Christmas together."

Winter inhaled deeply, almost like she was absorbing his positive thinking into every cell. "I love—"

"Dar…are you…th—?"

"I love you!" She yelled the words with the hope they'd make it through the staticky line.

"Win…hel…o…be…sa…I…"

She was losing him but didn't want to release her grip from the steering wheel as she climbed steadily up the mountain. She smiled as he continued to communicate in syllables for another thirty seconds or so before the line was lost.

The smile didn't last for long.

Snow was piling on the road at an alarming rate, coming down so quickly she felt like she was in a *Star Trek* scene when Captain Kirk commanded the ship to move at warp speed. She'd never seen anything like it.

"Slow and steady."

Forty minutes later, she arrived at the cabin and gratefully pressed the button to open the garage door. Once inside, she had to practically pry her fingers from the steering wheel and open and close her mouth to unlock her jaw. The muscles in her neck and shoulders screamed when she attempted to stretch but began to loosen up by the time she carried her purchases inside.

Squeeeak.

Winter froze in the kitchen, listening closely to the sound that seemed to have come from just beside her ear. Turning in a full circle, she peered into every dark corner. Nothing stirred.

Stop being silly.

Returning her attention to putting away the groceries, she frowned at the half gallon of milk already in the fridge. Taking it out, she checked the expiration date. *Sell by December 28.* That meant the milk was fairly new and was nearly half empty.

Winter opened the cabinets to find bread, jelly, and yes, peanut butter. A large box of saltine crackers and several sleeves of cookies also sat on the shelf along with a box of cereal.

Odd.

Had Mrs. Ralston simply forgotten to take it with her, just as she'd forgotten to do several other things?

Closing the cabinet, Winter studied the dirty dishes in the sink. Maybe Mrs. Ralston had spent the night in the cabin, bringing enough food for a quick breakfast and lunch while she cleaned.

"Then something happened." Winter was liking this theory. "A family issue, or she might have gotten sick and needed to leave right away."

As Winter pondered the mystery, she pulled on a pair of gloves and carried the cleaning supplies into the master bath. Using an abundance of foaming cleaner, she sprayed down the sink, toilet, shower, and bathtub, then used the new sponge she bought to give every surface a good scrub.

Tossing the wet gloves on the towel bar to dry, Winter used a fresh towel to mop the sweat from her forehead before heading into the bedroom to change the sheets. Pulling off the soft duvet comforter and blankets, she ripped the sheets off, tossing everything into a pile to be washed with extra hot water.

Squeeeak.

Arms filled with linen, Winter stopped short a few feet past the bedroom door, heart thudding in her chest. The wind whistled outside as the storm picked up speed. The sound was most likely a limb sliding across a window.

Yes, that must be it.

Relieved, Winter headed to the laundry room, laughing at herself. "'Twas the night before Christmas Eve, and all through the cabin, weird sounds were making Winter Black turn into a crazy woman."

While the first load began to wash, Winter decided to take a break. She was tired and hungry, and with a start she realized she hadn't eaten anything all day except for the few bites of apple turnover.

"Food. Must have food."

Her phone caught her attention. Peanut butter and jelly always went better when she was binging a show. Which circled her back to one thing.

Wi-Fi.

Cell in hand, Winter headed into the garage and to the closet Mr. Mills had told her about. Spotting the breaker box, she was still wondering if keeping the router this far from the main living space was clever or silly when she opened the cabinet door.

It was completely empty.

5

After searching through every cabinet and drawer in the garages for the router or anything that might work as an internet connection, Winter was back on the leather sofa, this time with a fingernail between her teeth.

Seriously? How had her life gone from fa la la la la to fu—

Squeeeak.

Winter jumped. What in the fa la la was that sound?

Pushing to her feet, she began to pace around the great room, scowling at her reflection in the glass. Not only was she frustrated, but she was sick of jumping at every shadow and noise that went bump in the night. Had Montana not only stripped her of the bright and shiny Christmas she'd been anticipating but also stripped her of her courage?

No. She refused to let that happen.

Stalking over to the cabinet that probably possessed some fancy name akin to chiffonier, Winter opened the door and inspected the sound system. It streamed music, of course, which did her zero good without an internet connection, but there was also a stack of CDs in the back corner.

When Winter spotted a label called "Christmas Classics," she snatched it up and thrust the disc into the opening.

"You're going to have a good Christmas whether the universe wants you to or not," she muttered and pressed the play button, smiling when the familiar notes of "It's the Most Wonderful Time of the Year" filled the room.

Finding the remote and instructions for the gas fireplace, Winter was soon smiling at the dancing flames. A few taps and scrolls on the tablet had dimmed the lighting to the proper mood.

Swaying and singing her way to her box of decorations, Winter sang at the top of her lungs as she pulled out one of the antique angel ornaments and turned in a circle, spying something that made her smile. The Ficus tree!

Setting the ornament carefully down, she rushed over to what she guessed was a seven-foot tree, pushing and shoving the heavy thing from the corner to just in front of a window. Perfect.

Well, not perfect, but good enough.

A string of white lights later, the Ficus appeared more *Charlie Brown Christmas* than anything, but Winter was determined to keep going.

"Jingle Bells" had taken over the sound system by the time she placed the antique glass star she'd found while shopping with Autumn on the top branch. The tree didn't want to hold it, so after a search through the garage, Winter found a long dowel sturdy enough to support its weight.

When she was finished, she stood back to take in her makeshift masterpiece. And laughed.

It wasn't all that bad, actually. The tree was bright and shiny all right, and she'd done the best under the situation she'd been given. More than anything, she was still smiling as she watched the twinkling lights.

"Ain't no stinkin' blizzard getting me down."

The thought of the snowstorm outside caused the smile to slip a little. Would Noah and her grandparents make it tomorrow? Or would she spend Christmas Eve and even Christmas all alone?

Somber once again, not even "Joy to the World" lifting her spirits, Winter wandered back to her phone. "Please have one bar."

It didn't, of course. And now the battery was nearly dead from where it had been frantically searching for a signal to link up to. Grabbing her charger, she spotted an outlet and connected the device to charge. Not that it did her much good right then, but watching the little lightning bolt appear over the battery made her feel a little bit better. At least not quite so isolated and alone.

The device wasn't the only thing running on empty. She had completely forgotten about her hunger while decorating the tree. Winter's stomach growled, and her tongue felt glued to the roof of her mouth. She headed to the kitchen, glaring at the dirty dishes still in the sink.

"What shall my Christmas Eve Eve's dinner be? Ham and cheese or peanut butter and jelly."

Winter regretted that she hadn't had the foresight to have the grocery service deliver all her supplies today. But she'd been worried that her flight might be delayed or she'd have trouble finding the cabin and hadn't wanted to miss the delivery. It had seemed reasonable to have the large shipment of groceries delivered tomorrow. But now?

"Stop it. Think pleasant thoughts."

At least that's what her former therapist had told her. *"Count your blessings."*

Closing her eyes and rolling her head on her shoulders, Winter couldn't think of one.

Being in the middle of so much snow would be fun if

Noah and the others could be with her. Noah had even promised to help her learn to ski while here. But now?

Being off the grid would be nice at just about any other time of the year. But now?

Squeeeak.

Winter didn't even jump that time.

The wind howled hard enough to rattle the windows, and there was already what appeared to be several inches of new snow. Striding to the foyer, she shoved her feet into her boots and opened the front door. Stepping onto the porch, she braved the cold long enough to check whether her theory was correct about a tree branch making the terrible noise. When she didn't see a nearby tree on this side of the cabin, she gave up but took a quick look at the snow gauge she'd spotted earlier.

Four inches already.

A memory surfaced of Winter and her brother building a snowman together so many years ago. Justin had been about five at the time and was practically jumping out of his skin with excitement.

"What are we going to name him?"

The words had been heavily lisped because Justin had recently lost his top two teeth. He'd been adorable, and on that day at least, she hadn't been able to stop smiling each time he grinned at her.

"Your choice, bud. This snowman is all yours."

Justin had practically vibrated with excitement. *"Let's call him Mr. McFlurripotamus."*

He'd found his idea to be hilarious, but Winter hadn't been all that surprised. Justin had been at the age where he was obsessed with hippopotamuses, or hippopotami, as he'd insisted to be the "proper Latin plural."

Justin hadn't been wrong. The boy had been smart as a whip, curious and forever asking scientific questions that would have never occurred to her. That had been their last winter together before Douglas Kilroy stormed into their lives and stole it all away.

A shiver nearly rammed her teeth together, but she stayed outside long enough to gather up a handful of snow. It crumbled when she attempted to form it into a ball. She'd heard how dry the snow was in Montana but was still surprised when it appeared to be more powdered sugar than the icy sludge she was used to.

"No snowman making for me."

She took a bite of the snow, feeling like a little girl as the flakes melted on her tongue. It tasted fresh and clean, and she wished Gramma Beth were here to make her a big bowl of snow cream with extra vanilla, just the way she liked it.

A gust of wind rocked Winter back on her heels, a solid reminder that she needed to go back inside. A glance at the oversized thermometer confirmed that the brutal cold wasn't a figment of her imagination. Nineteen degrees was ridiculous.

"Stop complaining and stop feeling sorry for yourself."

Back in the cabin, she kicked off her boots and went straight to the gas fireplace and held her frozen hands straight out. The warmth was immediate, causing her frozen fingers to burn and sting. The pain felt good, though. A reminder that she was alive, and with life there was hope.

Her stomach growled, reminding her that life also needed to be sustained.

Once she felt properly dethawed, she wandered back to the kitchen and went through her meager selection of food. "Ham and cheese it is." To make the dinner more palatable, she spread butter on the bread and grilled her sandwich to golden perfection, wishing she had tomato and lettuce. Mayo too.

Back on the leather sofa, sandwich almost to her lips, a

sound caught her attention. Winter paused, listening harder before setting her dinner back on its plate.

What was that?

Snatching up the tablet, she cut Bing Crosby off in the middle of "It's Beginning to Look a Lot Like Christmas," and stood.

Scratch. Scratch. Scratch.

"I swear to God and all living things, that if there are mice in this cabin," she air quoted the word because calling this massive place something so humble still felt wrong, "I'm out of here, blizzard or no blizzard."

Scratch. Scratch. Scratch.

Winter followed the sound. Her socked feet were silent on the wood floors, and she forced her respiration rate lower so that the sound of her breathing was as quiet as possible.

Scratch. Scratch. Scratch.

The noise grew louder, more frantic. Another sound followed.

Was that what she thought it was?

Peeking through the glass door was the only confirmation she needed.

Meow.

Winter pulled open the door to find a yellow-and-white tabby turning in circles. Its meows became more urgent, more akin to a howl.

Squatting, Winter held out her hand to the frozen feline. "Hey, kitty. I bet you're cold."

The cat howled again and came closer. A cold nose touched the tip of Winter's finger just before teeth sank into her flesh. The tabby didn't let go when Winter tried to yank her hand away. Instead, it tried to pull her onto the porch.

"Ouch!"

When Winter freed herself from the cat's jaw, she

inspected her finger. Imprints were left, but the bite hadn't broken skin. "No rabies shots for me this Christmas."

The cat lunged toward her again, but instead of trying to bite her this time, the tabby sank its teeth into the hem of Winter's jeans. The cat pulled, its claws scraping into the porch with the effort.

He was clearly trying to tell her something, but what?

Squatting back down, Winter spoke soothing words to the frantic feline, even daring to stroke the cat's back, being careful of its teeth.

On the underside of the cat, even through the long fur, Winter spotted elongated and pronounced nipples. He was not only a she, but she was a momma.

Wasn't it a little late in the season for kittens? Apparently not.

The cat took a mouthful of Winter's sweater and pulled, claws scrabbling at the wood porch in desperation to get Winter to follow.

"Okay, Momma, I get it now. You need me to help you save your babies."

The cat paced, turning in circles as Winter slid her feet into her boots and pulled on the heavy winter coat. By the time she'd gotten the wool hat and heavy gloves on, the tabby was howling again.

"I'm coming. I'm coming."

Grabbing a flashlight she'd spotted earlier, Winter stepped onto the porch just as a gust of wind nearly knocked her over. The cat disappeared down the steps, then turned and waited for Winter at the bottom.

"It's beginning to look a lot like screw this..."

But Winter followed. How could she not?

6

Winter hadn't known that cold like this existed, but she knew it now. She also knew that the teens she was experiencing at that moment wasn't even the worst it would get on this mountain.

The cat didn't appear to notice the frigid temperature, though, even as her little legs sank into the snow up past her belly. She was on a mission, dragging Winter along with her.

At first, Winter had been afraid that the cat would lead her toward the woods, but she had turned the corner at the end of the garage, heading toward the back of the cabin. The momma would sprint ahead several feet before halting, staring at Winter with glowing eyes until she caught up.

"Don't judge me," Winter muttered at the cat who'd started howling again. "I'm doing the best I can."

Snow was like bullets on her exposed face, and she'd turtled her neck into the coat as far as she could manage. It didn't help much. Because she had already packed so heavily, Noah was bringing their ski clothes, including the balaclava that would have been extremely helpful right about then.

As they rounded the back of the house, Winter was

second-guessing the wisdom of this mission. Her teeth chattered, and her hand shook so badly that the flashlight beam jerked back and forth. Not that the light was very helpful. Instead of stabbing through the dark, the light bounced off the wintery confetti, reducing her visibility to less than two feet in front of her.

When the cat turned right toward the woods, Winter paused. This was stupid.

As much as she wanted to help the cat and kittens, Winter knew she'd be no help to anyone if she got lost and ended up dead herself. And though she hadn't experienced near blizzard conditions before, she had heard stories of how easy it was to get turned around, losing all sense of direction before freezing to death only feet away from shelter.

Her heart and mind warring with each other, Winter was torn between what to do. Go back, staying inside the house, ensuring her own safety. Or follow a cat into the great unknown.

The momma came running back, her expression as imploring as the sounds coming from her mouth. *Please*, the meows seemed to say. When Winter still didn't move, the feline came closer and lifted her body until her front paws pressed on Winter's jeans.

Yellow eyes practically begged for Winter's assistance, but there was something beneath the gaze. *Trust me.*

Bending low, Winter stroked the furry head growing stiff with a mixture of snow and ice. Even on vacation, she was a special agent with the FBI.

Fidelity - Bravery - Integrity.

Winter was proud of what the Federal Bureau of Investigation stood for, even when, at times, she loathed the restrictions wearing the badge created. Badge or no badge, she had a duty to others, and this desperate animal wasn't less deserving of her very best.

"Let's go."

As if understanding the words, the cat hopped away. Trudging behind it, Winter twisted her foot with every step, attempting to make the places where her boots sank into the snow extra large. Maybe, just maybe, she'd be able to find her path again that way.

After what felt like hours but had probably only been minutes, Winter came to a building she'd label a shed. The cat was gone but soon reappeared in a broken window.

"Smart kitty."

Surprised to find that the door wasn't locked, Winter was forced to yank the outward swinging door hard in order to get it past the piling snow. When the space was wide enough for her to get inside, it was a relief to be away from the driving snowflakes.

Not giving Winter even a second to enjoy the shelter, the cat jumped up on a shelf, howling just a few inches from Winter's face.

"Okay, okay." Winter reached out and brushed some of the snow from the cat's head and ears. "Where are your babies?"

As if she understood the question, the momma jumped from the shelf and over to a workbench that didn't appear to have been used for many years. Clearly a gardening shed, the small building housed a lawn mower, leaf blower, and weed eater along with an assortment of tools to trim bushes and small trees.

The cat, of course, had sought shelter in the very back corner of the space. Her eyes glowed an eerie green when Winter cast the light in that direction and began heading her way.

Mew, mew, mew.

A chorus of little cries got louder as Winter grew closer, and she found a tight bundle of furry kittens snuggled against what appeared to be a fairly clean looking quilt. The babies began to walk on unsteady legs, but their eyes were open. That made them, what, two or so weeks old?

Winter hadn't grown up with animals, so she wasn't sure. Not that it mattered. No matter their age, they were simply too little for the type of cold expected tonight.

At their insistent cries, the momma cat settled down and her hungry little army began nuzzling closer, fighting over who got to nurse first. The biggest, a yellow-and-white striped butterball, got to the momma before the others, nearly attacking her in a way that made Winter wince.

"Poor momma."

Counting five more, Winter watched until they were all settled in and nursing like little champs. Momma cat lowered her head and closed her yellow eyes, exhausted. If it hadn't been freezing in the shed, and if she still didn't need to find a way to carry the little family inside, she would have enjoyed witnessing the cozy little picture they created.

Heaving a sigh, she investigated the area, hoping to find a box or other container to create a makeshift bed. After opening every cabinet, though, she didn't have much luck with that idea.

Moving back to the blanket the kittens were using, she decided the blue-and-white quilt might be her only solution. She would bundle them in the center and carry them like a sack.

After giving the kittens a few more minutes to nurse, she began tugging at the quilt. Momma cat lifted her head, giving Winter a "who dares disturb me" glare. She'd apparently forgotten that Winter was out here freezing her butt off at her highness's not so subtle request.

"Don't you want to be nice and toasty in front of the fire?" Winter lifted an eyebrow at the feline. "I've got ham and milk too."

The cat stood abruptly, six little kittens hanging off her nipples like ornaments on a tree until they each lost their grip and fell back to the blanket.

"That wasn't very nice."

The cat licked her paw, clearly unconcerned as the kittens jittered around on wobbly little legs, their heads much too big for their bodies. Winter stroked a finger down a gray-and-white striped back before lifting the baby to the side of the blanket. The other five kittens were soon moved to join their sibling.

Winter tugged at the blanket, but it seemed to be stuck. Moving to the end, she tried again. Still stuck. Bracing her feet, Winter pulled with much more strength and managed to free several inches of the cloth.

"What's holding it down?"

Even through the heavy gloves she wore, her fingers felt like they were made from ice as Winter wound the free corner of the blanket around her hand, giving herself a much better grip.

"Come on."

If this didn't work, she'd give up and tuck the kittens inside her shirt. With a final pull, the quilt came free, causing Winter to stumble backward several steps.

Gasping, Winter stared in disbelief at what had been trapped beneath the beautifully quilted blanket.

Two lifeless eyes stared back.

7

After the shock of discovering a body had worn off a little, Winter's training kicked in and she ran through the list of everything she knew she needed to do.

Check for signs of life.

Even though the woman before her was most clearly and sincerely dead, Winter pulled off a glove and pressed two fingers to her neck. Skin the same temperature as the snow outside nearly burned into her flesh.

Inhaling deeply, Winter couldn't catch even a hint of the telltale scent of decay, and neither could she tell at a glance how long the woman had been dead. Though she wasn't anything close to a medical examiner, Winter thought that the frigid temperature and low humidity had combined to leave the body relatively unscathed from typical decomposition.

Call it in and secure the area.

Winter snorted at the first guideline and frowned at the latter, deciding that closing the door against the blizzard outside was just about the best she was going to do. She wished she had her phone with her so she could take pictures, but present circumstances didn't give her many options. Instead, she examined the corpse, committing each detail to memory.

White female in mid to late forties. Light brown hair cut at shoulder length, wearing jeans, a flannel shirt, and brown hiking boots. No rings on her fingers or other jewelry of any kind. No coat, purse, or other identifying objects to be seen.

Stooping low, Winter searched for any sign of injury, and without touching or rolling the body, nothing apparent stood out. She was loathed to move the poor woman, preferring to leave that task to trained examiners.

This was a crime scene, after all. Unless this lady had decided to roll herself up in a blanket like a burrito and toss herself into a freezing shed to die, this was murder. At the very least, she could have died of natural causes, and someone moved her here. Charges along the line of abuse of a corpse was a misdemeanor at the very least, depending on the circumstances and judge.

What had killed her, though?

That question would need to wait to be answered because Winter had no intention of interfering with a crime scene any more than she already had. She could already imagine the looks she'd receive from the local medical examiner and detectives.

Plus, she had bigger questions she needed to address right then.

If the woman's death wasn't due to natural causes, who had murdered this poor woman? And was the killer or killers nearby?

Laughter echoed in her head, and Winter whipped around, her hands up in defense position. No one was there.

More shaken by the phantom sound than she'd been by the discovery of the murdered woman, Winter took in the deepest breath she could manage without coughing.

Exhaling the air from her mouth in a cloud of vapor, she fought to compose herself.

Pull it together.

After another moment of deep breathing, Winter's hands no longer shook. Of course she'd be jumpy after finding a body so unexpectedly. And of course, finding said body would resurrect memories of her baby brother, notorious serial killer Justin Black, or any of the madmen she'd stopped from harming others since first joining the Bureau.

And there were many. Too many. And even more still wandering the planet untouched by the hand of law.

Was one of them currently on this one acre of land?

She would have been made of stone to not be at least a little upset about her current circumstances or a robot not to have her body react to the distress it clearly felt. As much as she had wished she was both of those things at times, she wasn't. She was flesh and bone, heart and soul. Alive and breathing. The things the woman in the blanket no longer was.

Why?

Winter shivered so hard her hair whipped into her face. The rush and heat of adrenaline was wearing off, reminding her that she needed better shelter than this metal building with its broken window could ever provide. One thing was for sure. If she didn't get herself and these furry little beings back into the cabin, she'd wouldn't live long enough to figure that out.

Draping the edge of the blanket back over the woman's face, Winter made her a silent promise to be back and make sure the area authorities returned with her.

"We'll find out who did this to you."

Winter didn't add the two words ringing in her mind...*I promise.* She'd learned at the beginning of her career that those were two of the most dangerous words in the world, not only to the people she said them to but to herself.

Momma cat rubbed against Winter's legs with another sound that was more howl than meow. The feline appeared to be agitated, undoubtedly wondering why this human wasn't doing what she was supposed to be doing...saving her babies.

Winter studied the area again. Other than the quilt she could no longer touch, there wasn't anything else she could use to bundle the little family up with.

"You ride with me, little ones."

After making sure her shirt was firmly tucked into her jeans, Winter scooped the kittens up one at a time and stashed them down the collar, gasping when the cold pads of their feet touched her warm skin. When all six were in place, mewing and wiggling against her belly, Winter zipped her coat back up as far as it would go.

Momma cat headed straight for the door, her yellow-and-white tail straight up in the air. At the entrance, she glanced back and meowed in a way that clearly articulated her thoughts. *Let's go.*

"Yes, ma'am."

Needing to secure the crime scene the best as she could, Winter shoved at the door, her head bent to protect her face from the driving snow. The wind was even gustier now, the white stuff blowing sideways as it fell down in sheets. In the short time she'd been in the shed, an additional couple inches had fallen, making the process of closing the only entrance more difficult than opening it had been.

Gripping the handle, Winter noticed something. The lock was broken. Recently or long ago, she wasn't sure, and she didn't have time to examine it more thoroughly. She could only handle one problem at a time, and her most urgent issue was that she needed to get out of this cold...now.

Using her shoulder to shove the door closed against any wild animals that might be eager to feast on a free dinner, Winter was thrilled to see that the footprints she'd made on the way to the shed were still there.

Tempted to try the back door, Winter reasoned it would most likely be locked. She didn't want to waste time or risk the possibility of getting turned around in the near zero visibility conditions. With six now warm bodies nestled against her stomach, she began the harsh plod back the way she'd come.

Pain burst through her skull so hard and unexpected, Winter fell to her knees. *Oh no. Not now.* Had the agony not been so great, she might have laughed at her attempt to banish the "gift" The Preacher left her with when she was only thirteen. Visions swam before her eyes, flashing as quickly as a strobe light at a disco.

Gunfire and men in gray uniforms falling to the ground.

Heavy breathing as someone scaled a fence.

The scream of a woman as she was yanked from her blue SUV.

Landscape flashing by a window.

Another harder burst of pain shot through Winter's head, and the warm drip of blood burned a trail down her lips and chin.

Running through woods.

Another scream as a woman wiping down a window was attacked from behind.

The snap of a bone as the woman fell through the boards of a porch.

Male laughter, loud and deep.

As the vision receded, the laughter faded more slowly from Winter's mind. A cold nose bumped her cheek before a rough tongue licked her chin.

Blood.

Winter jerked upright from where she'd fallen on hands

and knees into the snow and swiped a frozen glove under her nose. The ice and snow came away red. She wasn't even sure why she'd double-checked the source of the cat's curiosity. A nosebleed always accompanied one of her visions.

As the headache receded, Winter attempted to recall each of the elements she'd seen during those few seconds. Though she hadn't seen the woman's face in the vision, she didn't need to be a special agent to conclude that the body in the shed and the woman who'd been washing windows were one and the same.

The housekeeper?

It was the logical assumption, and Winter cursed the storm swirling around her for yet another reason. She had no means of communicating with the outside world to let them know of her grisly discovery.

Who was the man?

Pushing to her feet, Winter checked on the kittens, glad she hadn't fallen onto her stomach and killed them all. That would have most likely pushed her over the mental edge.

Taking a step forward, she went back to the question. The man in her vision. Who was he? Had the housekeeper known him and had been the victim of a domestic dispute?

Head down as she placed one boot in front of the other, Winter considered her earlier theory. At that time, she'd believed the housekeeper had spent the night or nights at the cabin, bringing just enough food to sustain herself while she relaxed in the luxurious environment. Or escaped an unhappy relationship?

It was possible.

Trudging forward, Winter could almost imagine the scene now. The couple'd had a fight, with the housekeeper coming to stay here knowing the cabin would be empty for a time. The man finding her here, killing her for daring to leave him again.

But what about the fence? Or the men in gray uniforms?

Winter was still pondering the questions when she found she'd retraced her steps all the way back to the front porch. Thank goodness. She felt like a human icicle.

Like the dead woman.

Winter shook off the thought and stomped the snow off her boots before opening the front door and stepping into the warmth. The fire glowed from the fireplace, seeming to call for her to come closer. The momma cat didn't wait for an invitation. She darted straight for the flickering flames before turning to meow a new message for Winter.

Hurry, the sound seemed to say. Winter wouldn't argue with that.

Stripping as quickly as her frozen fingers would allow, Winter left her wet clothes by the door. With hands that jerked with each shiver racking her body, she managed to turn the locks and secure the chain, unable to leave the entrance unsecured no matter how miserable she currently was.

Meooow!

"I'm coming. I'm coming."

On feet that felt like blocks of ice, she made her way to the fireplace, her face, fingers, and toes burning with the change of temperature as she moved closer. A basket of kindling sat on the hearth, even though the fireplace was gas operated. She dumped what must have been decorative pieces of wood and grabbed a small throw draped over an ottoman, placing it over the basket.

The moment Winter stepped back, momma cat jumped in the basket and turned three times before plopping on her side. Sinking to her knees, Winter scooped the babies out one by one.

Two had yellow-and-white stripes much like their momma, while one sported stripes in a mix of gray, black, and white. Another was solid gray, and the other two were a mix of yellow, gray, black, and white.

She would have loved nothing more than to pull up a chair and watch them wobble around on their unsteady legs the entire evening. But she had too much on her mind.

The storm.

The dead woman.

The man in her vision.

Pushing to her feet, Winter's stomach growled as she began to pace. Remembering the sandwich she'd been forced to abandon earlier, she strode over to the leather couch, and the plate still sitting on the table.

Freezing in place, Winter stared at her sandwich, her mind going back to when she'd heard the first scratch at the front door. Had she even had time to take a bite yet? No. At least, she didn't think so, and she certainly wouldn't have been capable of taking off nearly half of the sandwich in a single chomp.

Just like the sandwich was now.

Squeeeak.

Heart hammering in her chest, Winter lunged for her shoulder bag, scooping it up as she turned in a circle to canvas each corner of the room. Plunging her hand inside, she felt around for her weapons just as a new thought occurred to her.

The leather purse was too light.

Spilling the contents onto the floor, her fear was confirmed in a single glance.

Her stun gun...her mace...her Glock.

They were all gone.

8

Moving on instinct and fueled by an infusion of adrenaline, Winter bounded over the leather sofa and raced to the kitchen. She pulled open the drawer closest to the left of the sink where she'd spotted a set of kitchen knives earlier.

It was now empty.

Heart hammering in her chest, she pulled out another drawer to find that only the spoons were left. Drawer after drawer and cabinet after cabinet proved to be the same. Only blunt objects remained in the entire kitchen.

Someone was teasing her, she realized. Why go through the effort of taking some but not all the utensils when taking the entire tray would have been easier? Why not confront her earlier or even now, her gun in their hand? Why, if not to tease?

Toy.

Play.

Destroy, mentally at first. Then…?

Winter's brother's laughter rang in her ears, and she

fought not to raise her hands to block out the sound. It couldn't be him. Couldn't be Justin.

No. It wasn't possible.

Was it?

Racing back to where she'd tossed her shoulder bag, she sorted through the remaining contents on the floor, searching for her keys. There might be a foot of snow on the ground, but she'd take her chances in a warm automobile.

They were gone.

She glanced to where she'd plugged in her phone. It was gone too, charger cord and all.

Refusing to panic until all her options were systematically eliminated, Winter headed to the garage anyway. She knew the basics necessary to hot-wire a car, and if a vehicle ever needed to be illegally started, it was now.

All four of the Jeep's tires were slashed. This didn't surprise her. She also wasn't surprised to find that the toolbox she'd noticed earlier was no longer there.

Turning on her heel, Winter marched back into the house, anger edging closer to fear. If she couldn't flee, she would hide. She'd gather all the food she could hold and barricade herself in the master bedroom until Noah and the others arrived.

In a blizzard?

She gritted her teeth against her negative thinking. "For however long I need to." She practically spat the words.

Checking on the cat and kittens as she rushed by, she was glad to see the little family was comfortably nestled in their little bed. At least one thing on this terrible Christmas Eve Eve was going well.

Grabbing a table lamp, she yanked the cord free from the wall and headed toward the master bedroom, her head on a swivel. Every sense on high alert, she listened, her ears alert to any possible sound.

Where was her tormenter hiding? When would he grow tired of his game? What would he do next?

Creeping down the hallway, turning in a slow circle as she went, Winter barely inhaled a breath, afraid the noise would disguise the sound of her opponent's movements. Reaching the open doorway of the bedroom, she tightened her grip on the lamp, ready to swing if needed.

Instead of tiptoeing into the room, she dashed inside, hoping surprise would give her some small advantage. Lamp at the ready, she swung toward the inside corner, the only place her tormenter could hide.

Nothing.

With equally quick movements, she searched the entire master suite, not leaving a single corner untouched. This would be where she would hunker down for the duration. Now, she just needed to grab everything she might need for the next couple days.

"I can do that."

Hyper alert to her surroundings and ready to swing the lamp if needed, Winter moved back to the hallway. Since she'd already searched and secured the bedroom, Winter reached for the doorknob to pull the door closed behind her. The doorknob came apart in her hand. The piece on the other side fell to the wood floor with a loud thud, making her jump.

As she stared at the empty hole in the door, she simply couldn't believe it. In the space of time it had taken her to rescue the kittens, someone had been busy. Winter inspected the piece of metal in her hand. And the culprit thought of everything, including taking the screws so that she couldn't reassemble the lock herself.

"Methodical and organized," Winter could almost hear her best friend say. Dr. Autumn Trent was a forensic and criminal psychologist turned special agent for the FBI's Behav-

ioral Analysis Unit. *"Seeking power and control, this unsub fantasizes about having ultimate power and domination over his victims."*

"Elf that."

Even as she smiled at her own play on words, tears formed in Winter's eyes.

Only hours ago, she'd arrived at this beautiful cabin with her spirits high, excited to have the big family gathering she'd always longed for. Now, all hope for a bright and merry holiday was gone. Instead, Winter's black Christmas was getting darker by the second.

"Stop."

Her voice cracked, and she knew she needed to compose herself. With her mind emotionally hijacked as it was, she was close to mentally spinning in circles before she completely lost control and crashed and burned.

She needed to think. Calm down. Take a deep breath.

Squeeeak.

Heart like a racehorse in her chest, Winter spun toward the sound, and tried to pinpoint where it had come from. It had been louder than before, but what did that mean?

The wind was still wailing outside, so if the squeak was coming from a tree limb on the glass, wouldn't the sound be more frequent and consistent?

Filling her lungs with a deep, steadying breath, Winter didn't have time to puzzle through the questions right then. Instead, she took stock of her situation.

No communications were available to her, and all her weapons were gone. She was up against an unknown foe who appeared to enjoy mental warfare. Her only means of transportation were her own two feet, but with the driving snow and howling wind, leaving this cabin would be little more than suicide.

That left her with very few options.

She couldn't flee, and now she wasn't sure she could hide. Squaring her shoulders, Winter had one choice left. She'd have to fight. The thought made her laugh. Fight with what? She didn't even have a knife to bring to a battle against her own gun. She pictured herself brandishing a ladle in one hand and a spatula in the other.

Holding the lamp as if it were a bat, she headed back down the hallway toward the kitchen, testing doorknobs as she went. Each fell apart at her touch.

"Son of a nutcracker."

At least she still had a miniscule piece of her sense of humor left, and she was quite enjoying replacing curses with Christmas cheer. Whatever it took to keep her calm in the face of this dangerous situation.

Back in the kitchen, Winter opened the drawers until she found a cast-iron skillet. She smiled, thinking of Rapunzel in *Tangled*, one of Winter's favorite Disney movies. If the fair-haired princess could wield cast iron with such effectiveness, so could she.

Against a Glock?

Winter refused to let herself think about that. Instead, she had an idea. Opening other cabinets, she pulled out all the cast iron she found as well as any heavy-duty baking sheets.

Metal stopped bullets, and the standard magazine in her service weapon held fifteen rounds.

Winter laughed, which sounded more hysterical than she liked, now picturing herself as Wonder Woman. Maybe she could wrap baking sheets around her wrists and deflect bullets as they zoomed in her direction.

"Now, you're just being silly."

Rushing into the laundry room, skillet held at the ready, she picked up the two plastic laundry baskets she'd spotted earlier and ran back to the kitchen. She grabbed anything made of metal she could find and tossed them into one of the baskets. Maybe she could get lucky and sling a pan like a frisbee, striking her opponent in the throat and—

Out of nowhere, the cat jumped up on the counter in front of her, and Winter screamed so loud it hurt her throat. Flailing her arms, she stumbled backward, dropping the baking sheet in her hand as full-on terror dumped yet another load of adrenaline into her system.

"Sh...sugarplum fairy."

Hand over her racing heart, she stared into the yellow eyes that were, staring right back. "You scared me."

Momma cat licked a paw in response, completely unfazed by both the clatter of the pan on wood and Winter's reaction. Maybe after having off-season kittens in a blizzard, there was very little that could rattle the feline.

Bending to pick up everything she dropped, Winter hated to see how badly her hands trembled with the task. She wasn't acting very special agenty right then.

"This is different."

And it was.

As a special agent, she had her training and weapons as an advantage, but right now, almost everything useful had been stripped from her by a predator who appeared to enjoy playing with his food before taking a bite.

Except your mind.

That was the only reminder Winter required to begin gathering all that she needed again.

Food went into the second basket as well as all the spoons in the tray. She bagged all the ice from the freezer, knowing she'd need to keep the cold stuff cold because, if her plan worked, she might be in hiding for at least a couple of days.

Lugging both laundry baskets back to the master bedroom almost pushed her nerves to the breaking point. She needed both hands to carry each of the baskets, leaving her unable to wield the skillet. Winter made quick work of the task, and the cast iron was back in her hand as she gathered the kittens still snuggled down in their little bed and moved them in front of the bedroom fireplace.

Was there anything else she could use?

A final check through the garage and kitchen yielded a bundle of rope, a roll of duct tape, and a hammer that had fallen under a bench.

Rope coiled over her shoulder and duct tape on her wrist like a bracelet, Winter moved back into the house, hammer in one hand, skillet in the other. A part of her wished she'd thought to stuff a baking dish down her shirt as a makeshift Kevlar vest.

"Yeah…and you could place the metal strainer on your head too."

She choked on a half laugh at the image that created, even as she briefly considered the practicality of creating a suit of armor out of kitchen supplies.

Winter waited for the momma cat to enter the master bedroom with her before shutting the unlockable door. The cat settled back into the basket with her kittens while Winter shoved a heavy dresser across the room. Not stopping there, she pushed a chest of drawers in front of the dresser, followed by every other piece of furniture she could move.

With that task done, Winter swiped at the sweat rolling down her face and picked up her skillet again.

"Doorknob?" She used her best mafia voice. "I don't need no stinkin' doorknob."

At least, that was what she wanted to believe.

9

Winter's stomach growled, a reminder that she still hadn't eaten much of anything that day. She needed to keep up her strength while she could. She had a feeling her tormenter wanted to prolong her mental agony.

Setting the skillet down on the bed, Winter opened one of the loaves of bread. She had taken all the food in the kitchen, which she still hadn't decided was a wise move or thoroughly stupid.

Did she really think she'd starve her tormenter to death in a couple days? No. Would her reckless move only serve to make him mad? Most likely.

Did she care? Yes and no.

A part of her wanted him to just show himself and get this ball rolling. The waiting and wondering were almost more painful than a physical blow.

Almost.

Opting for peanut butter and jelly this time, Winter used a baking tray as a table and began assembling the comfort food.

Meow.

Glancing up, Winter met a pair of hopeful yellow eyes. She smiled at the tabby. "I haven't forgotten about you." Pulling out the pack of ham from where she'd stashed it in the ice, she pulled out a slice. "Here you go."

Momma cat snatched it from her fingers and began gobbling it whole in a way that emphasized just how truly starved she was. Poor thing.

This time, Winter broke off a piece, holding it out so the cat would eat a bit more slowly. When the slice was consumed, Winter took a glass and a bowl into the en suite bathroom, filling them both with water from the tap.

Setting the bowl down, she watched Momma drink while she took the first bite of her PB&J. She closed her eyes as the flavors melded together, taking her back to her childhood.

Her baby brother had always wanted extra jelly on his sandwich, which always ensured that great globs of the grape goo ended up on the front of his shirt. Justin would just smile and shrug, lifting the material to suck on the spot.

"Fixth ith." Justin had only been six years old when The Preacher had slaughtered their parents and stolen the little boy away. He'd been missing his front two teeth the last time she saw him, and his adorable lisp had given her plenty of fodder for teasing him mercilessly.

The punch of grief hit her dead center in the chest, and Winter closed her eyes against the familiar pain. It didn't help. This pain was brutal.

Thinking about that terrible night as she was experiencing another terrible one wasn't productive, but Winter couldn't seem to help herself. The memories insisted, refusing to be beaten away.

It had been a Friday night in October, and Winter had been excited to spend the night with her best friend Sam. They'd planned to binge-watch gory Halloween movies on the Syfy channel while stuffing themselves with extra-buttery popcorn and talking about boys.

Justin hadn't wanted her to leave him that evening. He'd held her close, smelling of baby shampoo.

"Night, Winter." She could almost hear his voice, even after all these years. *"Thleep tight. Don't let the bed bugth bite."*

Instead of squeezing him extra hard, she'd extricated herself from his pudgy little arms and dropped a quick kiss on dark hair still damp from his bath. *"G'night, twerp."* She hadn't even looked back on her way out the door.

It had been the last hug she'd ever get from her only sibling, and she regretted the teenaged callousness she'd shown to both him and her parents. She'd barely spared them a glance before leaving.

Over the years, she'd wished she could have turned back time. If she could have, she would have stayed home. If she had, though, she'd be dead. Butchered like her parents.

Counselors had told her countless times later, in their professionally soothing voices, that her absence from the house that night hadn't changed anything. A stranger, a psychopath, a serial killer, had targeted her family for some reason no one could fathom at the time, and Winter's presence wouldn't have made any difference in the outcome.

"Sorry, girlie. I'm not here for you. Just him." The Preacher's voice, quiet with a Southern accent, had been oddly sympathetic just before he'd nearly killed her.

She was fortunate to be alive, various people told her over and over. It got to a point where she'd just nod and let them think they'd convinced her their sentiments were true, though for many years, she'd wished The Preacher had killed her too.

As an adult, she knew her feelings were classic survivor's guilt, but she'd never forgiven herself for walking out the front door that night.

Winter's sleepover hadn't gone as planned, though. She and Samantha had argued over a stupid teenage boy, and she'd left Sam's house, walking down the windy, leaf-littered sidewalk at two o'clock in the morning.

Her house had been as quiet as this house was now as she'd crept inside, upset from the argument with her BFF and simply wanting to go to bed. On the way to her room, she'd been drawn to her parents' door by the dim light spilling from their room and into the hallway.

She remembered it all.

Red crosses drawn in their blood on the walls. Jude 14–5 written in the same bloody scrawl. It wasn't until later that she learned what the verse meant:

"Behold, the Lord came with many thousands of His holy ones, to execute judgment upon all, and to convict all the ungodly of all their ungodly deeds which they have done in an ungodly way, and of all the harsh things which ungodly sinners have spoken against Him."

She hadn't even been able to scream before she was attacked from behind, hit hard enough to cause a short coma and a lingering traumatic brain injury that had since proved to be both a blessing and a curse.

Douglas Kilroy had taken everything from her that night, but she couldn't begin to imagine all that her baby brother had experienced from The Preacher's guiding hand.

He had turned Justin into a monster more evil than The Preacher himself. A monster who killed and manipulated, thrilled and energized only when creating havoc and mayhem.

Very similar to the havoc and mayhem being thrust on her tonight. And the poor woman in the shed. The housekeeper, Mrs. Ralston.

Taking another bite of her sandwich, Winter moved to the side of the window and gazed out into the darkness, but the night was so absolute she couldn't see if the snow had slacked off at all. She felt it, though, felt the ice and wind on the other side of the thick cold pane of glass.

Reaching up, she felt for the lock, making sure it was closed tightly. It was, which almost surprised her more than if it too had been broken.

Her tormenter had simply been proving a point, she now believed. He'd wanted her to know how clever he was and that nothing she did would make a difference.

It was like he'd done something similar before.

After standing at the window for far too long, Winter shook herself and took the last bite of her sandwich. Downing the last of her water, she moved closer to the fire to sit beside the nest of kittens. The momma licked her fingers when she reached down to stroke a finger over each little head.

"Some rescuer I turned out to be, huh, Momma?"

The cat pushed her head into Winter's hand in response. The tabby reminded Winter of Autumn's fat cat named Peach, though this one was much sweeter than Autumn's orange ball of fur.

Would she ever see Peach again, or the snaggletooth Pomeranian mix named Toad? Would she live to see Autumn or Aiden or any of her other FBI peers? What about her grandparents? Noah?

Winter barely managed to stop the sob that wanted to escape from her lips when she thought of him. Noah Dalton was a hardened combat veteran and an agent of one of the most influential government agencies in the country. But he was as soft as a marshmallow with her.

Noah had experienced a fair amount of his own pain, she knew, but that hadn't changed who he was as a person. He'd gained that strength from his mother, the woman Winter was supposed to meet for the first time on Sunday.

What about Lucy, Noah's beloved older sister? Noah had told her endless stories about the two of them as kids, and she knew the siblings were still close although they didn't get to see each other that often.

Winter had imagined being pulled into both of their embraces, to have a new mother and sibling of sorts of her own.

Would any of that happen now?

"Stop it."

Momma cat's ears perked at the sound of Winter's harsh tone, and she stroked the soft orange and white fur in a silent apology. Winter received a rough brush of tongue on her palm in return.

"We're going to be okay," she told the purring cat, though the affirmation was more for herself. "Noah and the others will be here in a couple of days, and knowing him, he'll have some of the locals come here as soon as they can for a welfare check."

The tabby's ears pricked, her yellow eyes growing wide as she appeared to listen to something Winter couldn't quite hear. Goose bumps lifted on Winter's arms as the cat stood and shifted to stand over her babies.

Winter wasn't a cat whisperer, but she sensed the momma was scared.

"What is it, girl?"

Winter turned to look in the direction the cat had been staring. The closet.

"I've already checked in there. It's completely empty. I—"

The cat hissed.

Squeeeak.

10

A creeping sense of dread crawled up Winter's spine at not only the sound but the cat's reaction.

Something—someone—was coming. The cat knew it, and Winter could feel it too.

Her knees popped as she pushed to her feet, reaching for the skillet with one hand, the hammer with the other. Winter's ears began to pulse from listening so hard, and her feet seemed to shift back and forth of their own accord, as if urging her to run.

She didn't blame them. She wanted to listen to the survival instincts screaming at her and make a speedy exit. But where would she go, and what would she do once she got there? The exit to the hallway was barricaded by the furniture she'd moved against the door while the patio door was essentially barricaded by the blizzard. The bathroom doorknob had also been removed, so that direction was equally useless.

Moving to where she'd placed the two laundry baskets of goodies from the kitchen, she picked up the thickest baking sheet and forced it inside her shirt, tucking the hem into her jeans to keep her laughably ridiculous vest in place. It probably wouldn't stop a bullet, but it would surely slow it down, giving her a slim chance of survival. And all she needed was a chance.

Setting down the hammer, she hefted a can of green beans in her throwing hand. She remembered the time she and Noah had visited a slew of schools after a rash of shootings had the entire education system alarmed, not to mention anxious parents and students.

"If someone comes through your door with a gun, don't cower. Fight." Winter had picked up a book and a chair. She'd picked up book bags and even pencils. *"You are not defenseless, and if you have no other choice, throw everything you can get your hands on at the bad guy."*

She was about to practice what she preached.

In her head, he creak of the floor more closely resembled the report of a shotgun blast, but the sound hadn't come from her. It came from the closet.

How had he gotten in there? She'd checked every single corner before barricading herself inside this room.

Should she charge the door and surprise whoever was inside, or stand a few feet back, skillet at the ready? Should she—

Creak.

Fear was like a spider crawling on her skin, but the waiting, the wondering was so much worse. She needed to see the face of her tormenter. Needed to understand who she was facing. Needed to make absolutely sure it wasn't her brother, or god forbid, The Preacher come back to life.

As she watched, the doorknob on the closet began to turn, and though terrified, Winter's spinning brain began to slow as her vision pinpointed onto the immediate threat.

It was an inward swinging door. If it had been hung to swing into the master bedroom, she could have blocked it from opening. As it was, if she tried to hold the door shut herself, he could shoot through the wood, leaving her wounded or dead.

If she did nothing but wait by the side of the closet, skillet at the ready, he might lead with the Glock, and if that was the case, she might have a split second to disarm him before he was all the way through the door. But that was risky too. She had no way of knowing how he'd choose to come through the door. Slow? Low and fast? Gun turned in her direction or the other way?

So…green bean can or skillet?

She nearly laughed out loud at the limited options available to her, but she needed to be quiet so he wouldn't realize she was watching and waiting for him to come through the door.

He was taking so long and Winter's nerves were stretched so thin that she almost lunged forward and pushed open the door herself. Was he was waiting for her to do just that?

The person hiding in the closet had all the advantages. Was the prolonged waiting period part of his way of playing with his food a few minutes more? Or was he listening on the other side, trying to assess if she'd heard him coming?

What would it matter?

Her tormenter was sneaky, but had she been wrong? Had his deviousness come more from self-preservation than any joy he'd receive from toying with her emotions? Like a snake, was he as afraid of her as she was of him?

Then she remembered the dead woman in the shed.

No. More than likely, this person got an adrenaline rush while carrying out a dangerous crime. He was prolonging the rush, extending the pleasure.

This was his foreplay.

Winter didn't want to experience the main event.

Meow.

Winter jumped as the cat rubbed against her leg, and she very nearly shooed her away. Was that it? Was the man listening for her, trying to place where she was in the room and whether she was distracted? Had he come out of hiding because she'd been preoccupied talking to the cat and petting the litter a few minutes ago?

And if that was true, how would he know?

Turning in a circle, Winter searched the walls and ceiling but found nothing that even resembled the tiny eye of a camera. Surely the cabin's owner wouldn't install video cameras in such personal rooms. But what about the main rooms and the outside of the home?

It made sense. Her tormenter would have known exactly how much time he had to take her things and ransack the kitchen before cleverly removing doorknobs and whatever else he had planned. There wouldn't have been any need to hurry while watching her every movement.

The thought made her shiver even as her mind raced. Watched her from where? She'd searched every room when she'd been looking for the Wi-Fi router and hadn't found anything that even remotely resembled a computer screen.

She studied the closet door. It had been empty before, but it wasn't empty now. Could there be a hidden panel in the walls or floor she hadn't seen? A safe room with a hard line to the internet as well as at least one computer and a landline phone?

Winter needed to be in that room.

Meow.

Yellow eyes stared up at her, giving her an idea. If the tormenter was waiting on the other side of the door for her to be distracted, then she'd give him what he wanted. Clearing her throat, she began speaking to the cat in the lightest voice she could muster.

"We'll be okay, won't we, girl? I've got ham and milk, so don't you worry."

The doorknob began to turn, and Winter's heart threatened to burst from her chest as she pulled back her arm, ready to begin throwing everything she could get her hands on. She had to be quick and accurate too.

"You're such a good momma, you know that?" The door swung inward a quarter of an inch. "So brave to search for help and so smart to lead me to your babies. You should get a feline of the year award."

The cat had stopped rubbing against her leg and was staring in the direction of the closet door too. The momma hissed, her back arching, the hair standing on end.

Whatever was coming their way, the feline clearly didn't like it.

Neither did Winter.

A flash of a werewolf movie she'd gone to see when she was a teen came to mind. Half man and half wolf, with teeth the size of baby carrots had been a terrifying sight. That the beast had been driven to kill even when the human side of it fought against such crimes had left Winter sleepless for days.

People were like that too, she knew.

Good and evil. Yin and yang. Light and dark.

When the door didn't open any farther, Winter remembered that she needed to pretend to be distracted. But for the life of her, she couldn't think of a thing to say. Instead, one of her favorite Christmas songs popped into her mind.

"Silent night, holy night. All is calm, all is bright."

Though her voice was low and shaky, the door began to swing open again, tiny fractions at a time.

"Round yon Virgin, Mother and Child."

Winter caught a glimpse of a gray sleeve and prepared to launch one of her ridiculous one-pound missiles. She put her odds of winning this battle at about twenty percent, and that was being generous.

"Holy Infant so tender and mild."

Her throat was almost too tight to produce the words, but she fought through the stress and continued to do the only thing she could think to do…fight.

"Sleep in heavenly peace."

Praying tonight wouldn't be the last night on this Earth, she blinked away tears as her tormenter revealed himself more fully.

"Sleep in heavenly peace."

11

Winter launched the first can straight at the man's head, a roar of triumph on her lips as the metal smacked against his cheek. She didn't waste time on celebration, though, but launched a second can and then a third as fast and as hard as she could.

Bam!

The Glock exploded, but the bullet sailed way over her head, slamming into the wall behind her. One round gone.

She threw another can straight at the gun, managing to deflect the next shot far to her right. Two rounds gone. Thirteen bullets left.

Picking up the hammer this time, Winter slung it like a lumberjack would toss an ax into a tree. It was a good analogy because the man was big, even larger than Noah, with greasy black hair that hung in long strands down the sides of his head.

Though she'd hoped the hammer would impale the man's sternum, he still howled as the business side rebounded off his ribs.

He kept coming, though, the black barrel turning in her direction.

Bam!

The bullet whizzed past her ear, and she realized she'd done nothing more than anger the beast because he roared, his hand coming up to nurse the spot on his forehead where one of the cans had beaned him.

Twelve bullets left.

Eleven.

Ten.

As hard as she threw, he wouldn't go down. But he also hadn't hit her with a bullet, either. She'd call that a win…for now.

Sweating profusely, Winter threw her trusty lamp before reaching for a baking sheet. Another bullet zinged off the metal as it left her hands. That left nine.

Growing weaker, she steeled her strength, knowing she had no choice. She couldn't stop. She had to try. Had to fight.

Eight.

Seven.

Six.

Reaching down, Winter felt for her next projectile, but the basket was empty. Without hesitation, she lunged for the second basket of weapons only inches away.

The beast lunged too.

Winter landed hard on her back as his two hundred plus frame slammed down on top of her, knocking the breath from her lungs and crushing the baking pan under her shirt into her ribs. She tried to roll, stretching for the cast-iron skillet she'd almost had her hand on.

"No, you don't," he growled.

Jerked onto her back again, Winter couldn't move. The man's weight came down on her belly, making it even harder to breathe. His knees pinned down her arms, and even though she bucked in an attempt to get him off, he wasn't going anywhere.

The Glock made a reappearance, this time pressed into her cheek. A round was in the chamber, she knew, so it would only take the twitch of his finger for the next bullet to drive straight through her head.

Face bleeding from where a few of the flying cans had broken the skin, the man was a scary sight as he glared down at her. He became even scarier, though, when he broke into a wide grin.

"You're very pretty."

Winter had been shot, stabbed, kicked, and punched, but the pain of his obvious intentions hurt worse than any of those wounds.

"Get off me." She attempted to use her command voice, but the words came out weak and ineffective.

"Get me off first, and I will."

Winter gagged at the stench of the man as he shifted his weight. "You don't want to do this. I'm a federal agent. The entire FBI will come down on you if you hurt me even a little."

The smile didn't falter. "Tell them to say hello to my friends with the U.S. Marshals when they do."

Winter had noticed the logo on the pocket of the gray shirt but had been a little too busy to read it before. She read it now. Montana Bureau of Corrections.

Though he wore a corrections officer's uniform, Winter knew this man didn't work for a prison. An escapee? Winter had been too preoccupied planning the greatest Christmas in history to pay much attention to the news.

"When did you escape?" She needed to keep him talking.

"Last week. Piece of pie." The gun pressed harder into her cheek. "Don't plan on going back. You hear me?"

Winter nodded. "Yeah. What were you in for?"

The smile grew bigger. "Guess."

Bile rose in her throat, and she struggled to swallow it down. "I don't think I need to."

"Imagine how excited I was to have a pretty little thing practically delivered to me on a silver platter. It's been fun to watch you, mess with you a little."

Foreplay.

She'd been absolutely right.

Play to his ego.

"What's your name?"

The question seemed to surprise him, but he answered anyway. "Johnny. Johnny W. Russell."

Why did serial killers almost always use their initials?

"Well, Johnny W. Russell, I have people who will be looking for me very soon. What's your plan when they arrive?"

He didn't appear to be the least bit concerned. "Got the housekeeper's car stashed in the back. This house is getting a little old, anyway. Don't like to stay in one place for too long."

The gun moved to her throat. She swallowed hard against the pressure. "Smart. Where do you plan—"

He moved the Glock until the barrel pressed against the bottom of her chin, closing her mouth.

"That's enough talking."

Winter's heart started beating even harder than before. She couldn't let this happen.

"No," she managed to say.

He grinned. "I think I've heard that before."

Bucking with all her strength, Winter didn't care that the barrel was still pressed against her flesh. She'd fight until her last breath. She wouldn't go down easily.

A yellow ball of hissing fur barreled past Winter's head, launching straight into her captor's face. Johnny W. Russell screamed and fell onto the floor. Winter reacted without hesitation. She yanked her arms free and reached for the gun.

Bam.

Bam.

Bam.

Ears echoing with the blasts, Winter twisted the weapon, listening to Russell's finger break before he released his grasp. The cat was still clawing at his face and eyes, still biting at his nose as Winter rolled free, leaping to her feet, the Glock back where it was supposed to be. In her hand.

Two bullets left, and she wouldn't hesitate to use them on the madman. But first...

Rearing her foot back, Winter kicked her tormenter between the legs as hard as she could. He curled into the fetal position, moaning, and the momma cat leapt away. Her fur stayed on end, though, and she appeared ready and willing to attack again.

Good momma kitty, indeed. "Extra kibbles for you." Whenever she had access to any. But that was a problem for another time.

Grabbing the roll of duct tape, she didn't give the criminal even a second to recover from the blow before winding his wrists and ankles together. When he started cursing her, she wrapped a few layers around his head, muffling the sounds.

"Shhh...we're not cussing this Christmas."

Not completely happy with the duct tape, she pulled Russell over to the bed and used the rope she'd found earlier to practically make a mummy of him against one of the four thick posts.

"That should do it."

Backing away, Winter picked up the yellow-and-white tabby, holding her to her chest. She kissed the bridge of its nose and got a sandpaper lick in return.

Tears filled Winter's eyes as she stroked the momma's soft fur. "I saved you, and you saved me."

A gift for a gift. A life for a life.

Setting the momma cat back into the basket with her kittens, Winter explored the master closet and found the hidden door that led to the safe room she'd suspected to find. And as she'd also guessed, there was a landline, computer, and internet connection along with everything Russell had taken from the cabin.

After calling 911 and reporting the occurrence, Winter was cautioned that it could be a while before conditions allowed any vehicles through. After assuring the operator that she was safe and the prisoner contained, she called Noah. He answered on the first ring.

"Merry Christmas Eve, darlin'."

She glanced at a clock and realized he was right. For the East Coast, anyway. She still had an hour or so before Christmas Eve arrived for her.

Noah was quiet as she explained everything that had happened over the past twelve hours. He was shocked, enraged, and relieved in turn.

As he asked questions and she answered them, she heard him clacking away on a keyboard. He cursed softly, and she smiled. "Sweetheart, we're not cursing this Christmas."

She could imagine the confused expression on his face. She normally cursed more than him. "Okay. How about mother figgy pudding?"

It felt good to laugh. "That's much better."

He snorted. "Glad you approve. Now, what I was going to say is that the closest I can get to you is Bismarck, North Dakota in the morning. I'd need to rent a four-wheel—"

"Noah, that's crazy."

"What's crazy is you being attacked by a murdering

rapist. What's crazy is you still being stuck in an isolated cabin with him. What's crazy is—"

"Noah, I'm alive and well. Isn't that all that really matters?" She grinned. "Besides, I have a hero cat with me."

That seemed to take a bit of the steam out of him. "Yeah. So, what do you want to do about the holidays?"

Winter paced back into the master bedroom from the safe room to find Johnny Russell exactly where she'd left him. "I don't want to stay here, that's for sure, so I guess I'll just see what transportation is available and head home as soon as I can." Tears filled her eyes and she blinked them away. "It might not be until Christmas Day, though."

She desperately wanted to kick Russell in his jingle bells again.

"I've got an idea, darlin'. Give me a few minutes, and I'll call you right back."

Exhausted and thirsty, Winter left the safe room and began the process of pushing furniture away from the door. Though she was weary, she took the time to return the food back to the refrigerator since she didn't want it to ruin.

When the phone rang, she raced to pick it up.

"Hey there, darlin'. I spoke to a buddy of mine with the Marshals, and the locals have already been in contact with them. Looks like the storm should be out of your area by noon tomorrow, and they're looking to drop in on you by chopper. Locals will be coming by on snowmobiles too, so help is on the way."

Winter sagged in relief. There was a real possibility that she might be going home tomorrow. "That's good news."

"There's more. I called my mom, and she invited us to come and stay with her and Chris. They have the new house and plenty of room. She invited Beth and Jack, Autumn and Aiden too." There was a long pause, and when Winter didn't answer, he went on, "What do you think of that?"

Winter's throat was too tight to speak, so it took a few moments for her composure to return. Winter no longer needed her bright and shiny Christmas. Just being alive to celebrate the most wonderful time of the year would be enough...with people she loved and who loved her right back.

"I think that Christmas in Texas would be nice. Wonderful, in fact." She licked her dry lips. "But won't you be disappointed to not spend Christmas here? We've been planning it for months."

He chuckled, the sound deep and low. "We didn't need some fancy getaway, darlin'. Christmas is wherever you are. Don't you know that yet?"

She closed her eyes, counting her blessings. "I'm beginning to."

Momma cat rubbed against her legs, bright yellow eyes peering up at her. Winter stroked her soft fur and scratched under her chin.

Vixen. That could be the perfect name.

"Um, Noah?"

"Yeah, darlin'."

She grinned, her heart full as she imagined a very different kind of bright and shiny Christmas with the people she held most dear. It would be absolutely perfect there.

"Is your mom allergic to cats?"

The End

SPECIAL ANNOUNCEMENT
Back by popular demand, the Winter Black Series will continue with *Winter's Return*, the Second Season coming June 2022!

Thank you for reading.

All of the Winter Black Series books can be found on Amazon.

ACKNOWLEDGMENTS

How does one properly thank everyone involved in taking a dream and making it a reality? Let me try.

In addition to my family, whose unending support provided the foundation for me to find the time and energy to put these thoughts on paper, I want to thank the editors who polished my words and made them shine.

Many thanks to my publisher for risking taking on a newbie and giving me the confidence to become a bona fide author.

More than anyone, I want to thank you, my reader, for clicking on a nobody and sharing your most important asset, your time, with this book. I hope with all my heart I made it worthwhile.

Much love,
Mary

ABOUT THE AUTHOR

Mary Stone lives among the majestic Blue Ridge Mountains of East Tennessee with her two dogs, four cats, a couple of energetic boys, and a very patient husband.

As a young girl, she would go to bed every night, wondering what type of creature might be lurking underneath. It wasn't until she was older that she learned that the creatures she needed to most fear were human.

Today, she creates vivid stories with courageous, strong heroines and dastardly villains. She invites you to enter her world of serial killers, FBI agents but never damsels in distress. Her female characters can handle themselves, going toe-to-toe with any male character, protagonist or antagonist.

Discover more about Mary Stone on her website.
www.authormarystone.com

- facebook.com/authormarystone
- goodreads.com/AuthorMaryStone
- bookbub.com/profile/3378576590
- pinterest.com/MaryStoneAuthor

Printed in Great Britain
by Amazon